S0-AVC-699

Jenny Greenteeth

To Alexandra

Kids Can Press acknowledges the generous assistance
of the Canada Council and the Ontario Arts Council in
the publication of this book.

Canadian Cataloguing in Publication Data
Downie, Mary Alice, 1934-
    Jenny Greenteeth

ISBN 0-919964-58-3

1. Title.

PS8557.085J45 1984   jC813'.54   C84-098735-8
PZ7.D68Je 1984

Revised Text Copyright © 1984 by Mary Alice Downie
Illustrations Copyright © 1984 by Barbara Reid

All rights reserved. No part of this publication may be
reproduced, stored in a retrieval system, or transmitted
in any form or by any means, electronic, mechanical
photocopying, recording, or otherwise, without the
prior written permission of Kids Can Press Ltd.,
585½ Bloor Street West, Toronto, Ontario, Canada,
M6G 1K5.

Printed and bound in Hong Kong
by Wing King Tong

Book design by Michael Solomon

Kids Can Press Ltd., Toronto

84 0 9 8 7 6 5

Jenny Greenteeth

STORY BY
Mary Alice Downie

PICTURES BY
Barbara Reid

Kids Can Press · Toronto

Once upon a time there was a water witch named
Jenny Greenteeth.

She lived alone in a tumble-down old house in the Beaches beside Lake Ontario. She had been living there for so long that the walls of her house were crumbling and the windows were cracked.

All the children in the Beaches were frightened of Jenny Greenteeth. They were afraid of her blood-red eyes, her long tangled hair, and her slimy green teeth.

Jenny never bothered to look at herself, because the mirrors in her tumble-down house were cracked and she had only a single light bulb in each room.

Jenny wondered why no one ever came to visit her. Long ago when she had been a young water witch, children had come to play with her. She had taught them how to swim in the Lake and they had played water-tag.

Afterwards they would sit together on the shore. Jenny would dry her long hair in the sun and the smallest child would braid it with flowers.

But now no one came. Every Halloween she made bags and bags of seaweed candy, but no one came trick-or-treating.

Every Christmas she decorated the scraggly pine tree beside her front door with old tires and rubber boots from the shore, but no one came carolling. She hung a fishnet stocking by the chimney, but even Santa Claus didn't come.

And every summer Jenny hid between the rocks on the shore, waiting until the children came down to the water. Then she would pop out just as she had done years ago. "Does anyone want to learn how to swim?" She would grab the smallest child and laugh. "You can braid flowers in my hair. Won't that be fun?"

"Witch! Witch!" the children would scream, and the smallest one would burst into tears. Then they would all run away.

As time passed Jenny's feelings were hurt and she became cross. When the children ventured down to the shore, she would creep up behind and push them off the dock. She knew that the water was shallow and they'd just get their clothes wet.

"That'll teach them," she would chuckle, and she would eat another bag of stale seaweed candy to cheer herself up.

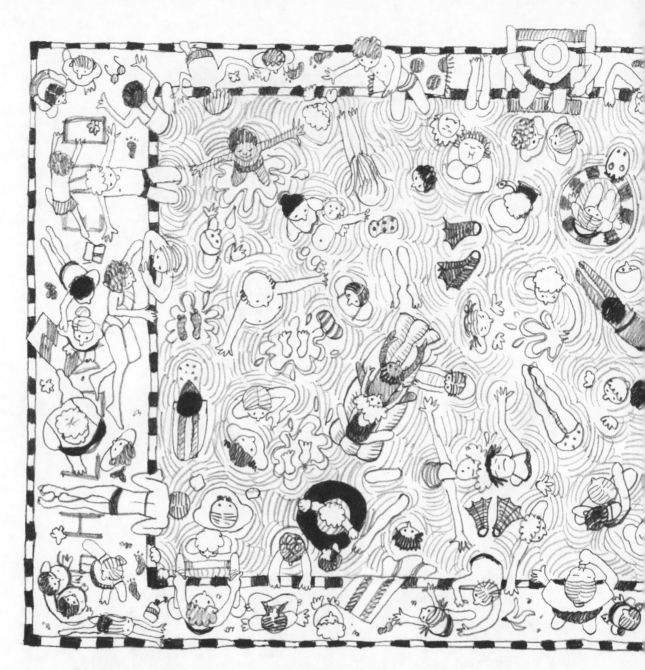

Soon no one came to the shore at all. The mothers and
fathers were so alarmed that a witch lived in the Beaches
that they forbade their children to swim in the Lake.

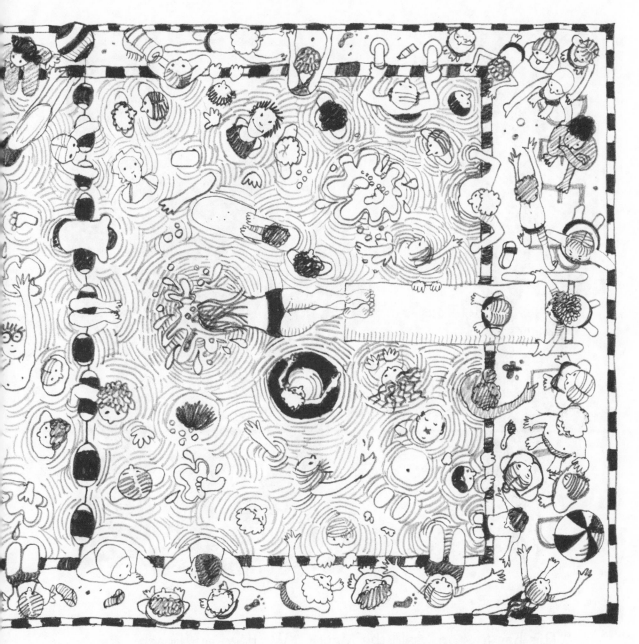

No one ever went swimming, except at the local pool and it became very crowded. Soon the pool was so crowded and dirty that it was no fun at all.

"This has to stop," said the Mayor. "We need our beach
back."

He went to see the Beaches policeman.

"You must capture Jenny Greenteeth."

"Not me," said the policeman, and he carefully locked himself in the Beaches jail. "That Jenny Greenteeth will push me in the water and I can't swim."

So the Mayor went to see the cadets. They were marching
up and down the boardwalk looking very brave.
"Will you capture Jenny Greenteeth?" asked the Mayor.

"No way," they said. They took off their jackets and pulled their baseball caps from their pockets. "Sorry we can't help, but we have a game in Mississauga today. Wish us luck."

In the end the Mayor sent the Beaches fire dog, a Dalmatian named Spark, to capture Jenny. When Spark came to the tumble-down house, Jenny was so pleased to have company

at last that she threw her a big juicy bone. Spark ran back to the Town Hall to bury it under the rug in the Mayor's office and forgot all about capturing Jenny.

Then the Mayor had an idea. He put a sign on the front door of the Town Hall.

Young David Smith saw the sign. He had just moved to the Beaches and he decided to go down to the shore to see this Jenny Greenteeth for himself.

When David reached the Lake, he hid behind a tree. At first he could only hear the waves breaking on the shore. Then he heard strange sniffing sounds. They came from behind a big rock.

David crept closer. He could see long grey hair all matted with weeds spread out on a rock and drying in the sun. He could see jagged fingernails combing the weedy hair.

David crept closer still. He looked around the corner of the rock and saw Jenny. Big tears fell from her blood-red eyes and he could hear her mumbling to herself.

David jumped back behind his tree. He had never seen a water witch before. What a horrible sight! David began to think about what Jenny had been mumbling. He thought and thought until at last he knew what to do.

He crept away, leaving Jenny still crying on the shore, and went straight to Queen Street. Then he went to see the Mayor.

David knocked on the door of the Town Hall.

"At last," said the Mayor. He ran to open the door and tripped over his long gold chain of office. "Oh, it's only a little boy," he said, picking himself up and opening the door wider. "What do you want?"

"I've come to free the town of Jenny Greenteeth," David told him. He held up a small paper bag.

"What? You? How can you capture Jenny Greenteeth?"

"I have a secret weapon," David said.

"I suppose it's a slingshot," chuckled the Mayor.

"No," said David. "I don't want to hurt her."

"Then it isn't a cannon?" the Mayor asked.

David shook his head.

"You'll see," he said.

He went down the steps and set off for Jenny's house. He was followed by the Mayor, Spark, and her puppies. Word spread quickly, and soon all the children of the Beaches, their parents, the cadets' baseball team, and the policeman who had let himself out of jail, were following too.

Jenny was sitting alone on her front steps. She had a watering can and a bag of cookies beside her.

"Who are you?" she snapped when she saw David walking
up the pathway. "What do you want?" She shoved a handful
of cookies into her mouth. "Don't you know that I push little
boys like you into the water?"

"Not this one, you don't," David said calmly.

"You'll be sorry if you stay here," Jenny warned, sinking her slimy green teeth into another marshmallow cookie.

"No I won't," said David. "Look! I have something for you."

"What is it?" Jenny asked crossly. "No one ever brings me presents."
David sat down beside her on the squeaky steps. Jenny edged away. "Leave me alone," she said. She pointed her jagged fingernails at him. "I'll turn you into a catfish if you're not careful."

David smiled and reached into his small paper bag.

"Here," he said. He pulled out a big red toothbrush and a tube of toothpaste.

"What's that?" Jenny asked. "It looks scratchy. Go away. I want to finish my cookies."

"Watch," David said. And he showed Jenny how to brush her slimy green teeth.

Everyone else watched from behind the fence. They couldn't believe their eyes. What kind of secret weapon was this?

Jenny took the big red toothbrush and dipped it into her watering can. Slowly she squeezed a blob of toothpaste onto the bristles. Then she began to brush her teeth. She brushed and she brushed, and as she brushed, her slimy green teeth began to shrink. In no time at all, they were a normal size and gleaming white!

Jenny Greenteeth looked quite different. She had such a dazzling smile that no one noticed the weeds in her hair or her blood-red eyes or jagged fingernails.

"There," said David. "Don't you feel better? Now you won't have to push children into the Lake to cheer yourself up."

"Just a minute," said Jenny.

She went into her tumble-down house and looked at herself in one of the cracked mirrors.

Then she came out onto her
sagging porch and glared at David.

"This is all very well," she said, "but no one ever
comes to visit me." She showed him the dusty sack of stale
seaweed candy in a corner of the porch. "Not at Halloween,
and not at Christmas." She pointed to the scraggly pine tree.

She glared out at the crowd of people who were watching
from behind the fence. "What am I supposed to do for
company?"

David leaned over and whispered in her ear.

Jenny laughed.

"Well, tell them," said David.

"Come here," Jenny commanded.

Slowly, nervously, the children and their parents, the cadets' baseball team, the policeman, and Spark and her puppies came towards her. The Mayor stayed behind the fence.

"I'm going to be the Beaches swimming coach," Jenny
announced.

"I'm going to give free swimming lessons to all the children
in town. You'll be Ontario champions in six months or my
name isn't Jenny Greenteeth."

She smiled her dazzling smile and everyone cheered — even
the Mayor. Spark barked loudly and ran up Jenny's steps.
She was hoping for another bone, but when she saw the
bag of cookies, she began to eat them instead.

Now Jenny had all the company she wanted. She gave swimming lessons every day from four to six o'clock.

Soon the Beaches Water Witches won every meet they entered. They travelled far and wide with their coach, Jenny, and of course, their toothbrushes.